THE FORBIDDEN RESCUE

"A Scottish Historical Time Travel Romance"

William Newell

© 2016 SubArctic Publishing

All rights reserved.

Disclaimer

This is a work of fiction. Names, characters, businesses, places, events and incidents are either the products of the author's imagination or used in a fictitious manner. Any resemblance to actual persons, living or dead, or actual events is purely coincidental.

No part of this publication may be reproduced, distributed, or transmitted in any form or by any means, including photocopying, recording, or other electronic or mechanical methods, without the prior written permission of the publisher, except in the case of brief quotations embodied in critical reviews and certain other noncommercial uses permitted by copyright law.

Stories In This Series:

Book One: Passage Through Time

Book Two: Return to Scotland

Book Three: The Forbidden Rescue

Book Four: Alone in Time

Book Five: One Last Time

~ William Newell ~

Dedication

"To all who long to live the romantic era.
This book was created for you."

~ The Forbidden Rescue ~

CONTENTS

Chapter 1: A Photography Job

Chapter 2: The Plaque

Chapter 3: Days Before Disaster

Chapter 4: The Lady and the Brute

Chapter 5: The Spy Exposed

Chapter 6: The Hotel Room

Chapter 7: The Day of the Bombers

Chapter 8: Home At Last

Book Preview

Chapter 1

A Photography Job

Dungallow, Scotland
March 9, 2019

Katie Duncan reviewed her work with great satisfaction. "Eaves are done!" She called out to her husband John.

The door to their little bungalow cottage was open, so he could hear her from the street. "Oh, excellent! Well done, dear."

Well done? She chuckled to herself. John was adapting to British ways of speaking quickly, as though he hadn't been born in America as she had. She teased him about it from time to time, always in fun.

Today was supposed to be a writing day, as had been the day before. However, though Katie's autobiography had sold exceptionally well- no doubt due to the many otherworldly and hardly believable aspects to her life story to date- it had only paid enough to pay the mortgage on their small town Scottish Highlands home through the approaching summer. John's photography was paying off, at long last, and that part of their income was bringing in bill and grocery money, if they stretched their pennies, or pence as it were. Frustratingly, just when she most needed to write even more to meet her obligations to her publisher and earn her next advance, she was running into a bad case of writer's block.

"Fancy a spot of tea?" She called into the hallway of the cottage, using her most dramatically terrible British accent. John was in the next room over, unseen, but reviewing his pictures online in the study where she normally worked. He peeked his head around the corner.

"Ha ha."

"Aye, rather and what not, pip pip."

"I'll just put the kettle on." He declared with a sigh, going into their kitchen.

"And make sure there's some lovely biscuits!" She demanded as she stepped into the front hallway.

"You mean cookies? Like these?" He picked up a plastic packet of cookies from the counter, leaned into the hallway, and threw it at her. She giggled and dodged, but grabbed them up from the floor.

"Oh, don't throw them down. That's wasteful. Hey, babe," she tried to sound optimistic while giving the bad news, but she was afraid of how he'd react all the same. "I don't think I'm going to write today."

"No?"

"No, and probably not tomorrow either. I'm going to wait until Tuesday, when I've had some time off. I've got the first few chapters done but... I'm just hitting a roadblock. You know?"

"Okay." He didn't sound too put out, though they both understood there was a major time crunch to get the first draft in within five months. A professional editor was scheduled to review the work by then. Every day counted.

"And, I was thinking I might come with you tomorrow, just for fun?" She offered her suggestion tenuously, knowing John was often very private about his photography, in particular paid gigs.

He coughed from the kitchen, then stepped back into the hallway. From his face, she could see he was clearly skeptical about the idea, but he put his arms around her anyway and kissed her on the forehead. "You sure that's a good idea? We've been trying not to get too much in each other's hair lately, I thought."

"We have, we have."

"It was your idea."

"I know." Katie admitted. "I've just been chained to the computer and I'm so bored with it. I need a break. I miss you, just being around you. I promise I won't be in the way."

"Of course you won't." He agreed, with an impish smile. "Because you're helping."

"Ah. Like an assistant?"

"Not like an assistant. Exactly as an assistant."

"Oh goodie." She shrugged and laughed it off. "Can I have my tea now?"

They found a seat in the living room. Neither had been tea drinkers growing up in America, yet it had become a custom they'd both enjoyed picking up.

Their first year in Dungallow had been emotionally challenging. Having twice travelled through time and connected deeply with the country, the couple had decided to put down roots. Their first journey had taken them to the time of the Caledonians, when Rome had threatened but failed to conquer Scotland. Katie still felt a kinship to her daughter and sister from that ancient era.

The second journey had whisked them both off to the Highland Clearances. Together, they'd managed to save the very town they were now living in, Dungallow. In that time period, John had been friends with a man named Buchanan. After their return, he'd developed a strong friendship with his descendent, Tim Buchanan.

"I suppose I should be more specific." He added, stirring his tea. "You'll actually be assistant to my assistant. Tim has asked to tag along as well."

"He doesn't work tomorrow?"

"Most people don't, you know. It's Sunday."

She slapped her forehead. "Of course. Right. Life of a writer."

"Life of a photographer. I can relate." He smiled.

After she'd finished her tea, she snuggled up to him and he put an arm around her shoulder. "John, is Clydebank near Cathcart? I'd like to visit, if there's time."

Cathcart, a small area within Glasgow, had been Katie's ancestral home. He nodded. "I think we can fit it in. We're meeting with the reporter and a historian for the shot. It should be an educational piece, if nothing else."

"Remind me, what's the subject?"

"It's the 78th anniversary of the German blitz that struck Clydebank. Not the biggest and most important anniversary, I suppose, since it's not the 70th or 80th, but still important. Paying gig, I'm not going to complain, you know?"

"Definitely!" She agreed. They sat in the quiet for some time after before he returned to sorting through photos and she took a shower. It was an ordinary spring day, one that would soon prove to be their last clear memory of peace and domestic tranquility before that Sunday.

~ The Forbidden Rescue ~

Chapter 2
The Plaque

Clydebank, Scotland
March 10, 2019

Katie was used to an unkind wind and sheets of rain, given she had grown up in the Windy City. Since the move, she thought she had even acclimated with some grace to the frequent downpours that were part and parcel of living on the storm-drenched Atlantic-facing coast of Britain. Even so, that morning's terrifying thunderstorm tested her expectations for weather.

They came out of the Highlands, the three of them and John's photography equipment, driving through the early morning horror show with their nerves frayed and their desire to shoot dampened. Tim Buchanan didn't show that he was rattled, though he was certainly nervous about John's driving. He offered twice to take the wheel, but John was having none of it.

"I know what I'm doing." He had protested, testily. "I've driven in worse snowstorms back home."

"Aye, but it's flat country, isn't it? Mountains can be different, you know."

"Are you sure the weather will be clear enough?" Katie had inquired.

"Definitely. This all blows over in an hour. We'll stop for coffee and breakfast, then get the work done."

"I really don't mind driving, mate." Tim had offered. Instead of replying, John had gritted his teeth and soldiered on. Katie was sure she'd never been more relieved to see Glasgow as they met with the increased, though not heavy, traffic that early Sunday morning.

They'd found a decent place for breakfast in Glasgow, a Mom-and-Pop operation that looked run-down, yet had a delicious smell coming from it. John and Tim opted for a full Scottish breakfast; eggs, fried tomatoes, Lorne sausage, toast, beans, and black pudding. Katie wrinkled her nose at the size of the meal, preferring her fruit and oatmeal.

"Good thing you're getting paid for this job." She chided John. Afraid she might sound scolding, she quickly added, "I'm not saying you haven't earned it, just, you know… let's not spend it all on breakfast, right?"

"Just this one off, of course." He agreed, happily dipping his toast into the egg yellow.

They had the restaurant much to themselves. Only a few locals were dining in corners off to themselves. After getting a refill, the slightly portly Scotsman leaned back in his chair and gave a great yawn. "I'll credit you. You got us here safe, friend. You've studied up on the blitzes, have you?"

John shrugged, thought about it some more, then nodded his head in the affirmative. "I've read the cliffs notes. Sounds as though it was a pretty grim time."

"It was at that. Over 500 killed in this town alone, another 1000 injured in the raid. They had a brief battle between a couple of gunners on a Polish ship and the Luftwaffe down by John Brown shipyard. Almost every building was struck by bombs. Nobody saw it coming that day, it being so far from the continent. I wouldn't want to have lived through that, I can tell you."

Katie smiled. "I can see you brought the right fellow with you for this."

The two men laughed. It was no secret that they shared a love of history, though Tim couldn't possibly know the amount of actual history John had lived through.

"But I don't entirely understand this, and maybe you can fill me in," Katie noted. "It seems like a place like this would have had some kind of warning. Surely the British knew they were coming."

Tim nodded. "It's true, they did know it and they prepared for that potential. The trouble is that some of the things they did to prepare either didn't work or worse. A few of their tactics, like the baffle walls raised to protect buildings, did more harm than good."

"Baffle walls?"

"Aye, these were walls placed in front of tenement entrances to protect them from bombings. But in some cases the walls were blown into the buildings and killed people.

It was… from what I've read of it, it was quite a sight. People were killed behind those walls, thinking they'd be safe, but the buildings were reduced to rubble."

"Dear God. Sounds awful." Katie replied, sadly.

"That's war. Ah, but we'd better tuck in, Duncans." Tim reminded them, checking the time. "You're supposed to meet with your reporter friend, isn't that so?"

"We are." John agreed.

Katie had no appetite left and simply pushed her bowl in front of her, opting to drink her coffee. "I'm ready when you two are."

They finished their meals in mostly silence, an even heavier atmosphere hanging over them than the one that had preceded due to weather. John was right though. The rain did stop and by the time they'd reached Clydebank, a city a long stretch to the west of Glasgow, the sun had even put in an appearance.

John phoned the reporter they'd arranged to meet, a woman by the name of Sophie. She gave them the address of yet another coffee shop and they met her there.

"I've got the list of places for you to shoot here." She said, giving them a notepad paper. "Addresses are here. I'll go with you to the first few stops, but I expect you'll take the rest of these on your own, right?"

"Not a problem." John assured her.

"Good. Normally wouldn't do this at all, but I need to see a few of the sights myself so I can do the descriptions. And I have an interview planned with a survivor at the third spot. That's where I'll leave you."

The band of reporters and photographers piled in the Duncan's car and drove off to their first stop, the site of a former tenement block. At one of the worst hit locations, only one of the buildings had survived the blasts.

"Every building was affected by the attack," Tim explained as they looked over the clearly rebuilt, replaced blocks of homes. "All but maybe seven or eight buildings. I had relatives who were killed here."

Katie looked up, surprised to hear this revelation. By the look on John's face, she could see it wasn't something he'd expected either. Her husband had been setting up his shot when he looked up, startled.

"Wow. I'm very sorry to hear it."

Tim waved him off. "It was before my time! I just know of it from stories. That's all. I'll tell you another thing." He added confidentially. "A lot more than 500 people were killed here."

The reporter, who had mostly ignored them and stood off to the side during their conversation, rolled her eyes. "You can't prove it."

"No, but there were enough people who came from the town and survived the bombs to say the low number isn't so. There were a lot more unaccounted for than the government wanted to be told."

She shrugged. "Let's get on with it."

She left them to their own devices at the site of the John Brown shipyard. A mostly empty stretch of land alongside the River Clyde had recently had a plaque placed alongside the walkway.

"Good lord. Look at all of these names." Katie commented, pointing to the lengthy listing of victims.

John traced his finger along the list, turning pale. "Oh geeze. I had forgotten. I had an Uncle... well, my grandfather's brother... who lived here in Scotland. That's his name!"

Katie looked down, finding the listing for one Arthur Duncan. "Honey, that could be anyone. I'm sure there was more than one Arthur Duncan in Scotland."

"Maybe." He sounded doubtful as he rubbed the back of his neck. "I always assumed he died in combat. We don't talk about it much in the family."

"Yes, I can imagine." Katie agreed. She could tell he was a little shaken by what he'd seen. She was about to console him, when she began to feel extremely tired.

"Oh no." She had time to mutter. "Feeling woozy John. You?"

"Yeah." The Duncan's were no strangers to this phenomenon, a weird blacking out that would lead them to a new time and place. But as they began to slip into the darkness, they were both momentarily surprised to hear Tim's slurred voice.

"What's happening to me?" He managed to say as his legs buckled under him.

Katie saw John gently place his camera on the ground as he carefully let himself fall back into the ground. For her part, Katie was already trying to sit when she felt the first hint of drowsiness. She barely had time to brace herself when the darkness overtook her and she couldn't reflect any further on what was happening.

~ The Forbidden Rescue ~

Chapter 3

Days Before Disaster

Clydebank, Scotland

March 10, 1941

John felt the heavy fog lifting and was looking down at his gloved hands. He found he was wearing thick overalls and in those gloves he appeared to be cradling an acetylene torch. Thankfully, it was turned off.

"Duncan!" A thickly-accented Scottish voice practically screamed in his ear. "Stop your lolly-gagging and get back to it, unless you want your pay docked. Same for the lot of you! You want to get paid today for actual work?"

"Yes, sir." He replied instinctively. He had no idea who the man was, but it was clear that whatever was going on, he had to answer to this fellow for the time being.

From prior experience in time travel, he knew he was now living the life of another person in the past. Whatever their profession had been, John was now skilled in that art. He'd been a fighter in Caledonia and knew how to wield a sword. During the Highland Clearances, he'd been a blacksmith in a small village. Looking about him, it now seemed he was a welder working on a ship. He expected he would be able to handle that job, no problem.

It was no great deduction gained by glancing about him to say that he was working in a shipyard, probably the same one he'd been about to photograph when he'd been sent to another time. Instead of open grassland, there was an actual destroyer being built and a large group of men scurrying about, finishing up construction.

That realization sobered him up. Judging by the clothing people around him were wearing, they had to be in the early part of the 20th century. He really didn't want to believe it was possible, but a sinking feeling in his gut told him he was likely there during World War II.

As before, he wasn't surprised he hadn't made the trip back in time with Katie right beside him. They'd been separated by miles, towns apart during the Clearances. He had to hope, though, that she wasn't too far off.

As he sweat in the heavy clothing, another thought struck him; hadn't

Tim been with them when they'd time-travelled? He'd have to keep an eye out for his friend. They'd all look like themselves, it seemed, and whether that was just by their own perception or if they appeared to wear different faces to others around them, he wasn't sure. He presumed that these ancestors whose lives they'd taken over simply looked like them.

As he was reflecting on past experiences, a dazed-looking red-haired man was strolling alongside the ship, getting screamed at by a supervisor for not doing any work. John smiled to himself; it was Tim.

"Sir! I'll talk to him. Give us a minute." He said, rushing to Tim's aid.

The supervisor scowled before giving them both a curt nod. "Five minutes, no more. There's a war on, or didn't you know?"

He hadn't known for sure, but that confirmed it. He took Tim by the arm and led him out into the sunlight.

"What is this? What is this?" Tim kept repeating. It wouldn't do to have the man freaking out any further, so as quickly as he could, John tried to explain the situation to the best of his understanding.

"Now we only have a few minutes before we need to get back in there and work. Follow my lead in this, and trust me. It'll all be fine."

Tim looked far less than certain about this assessment. "But why? It makes no sense."

"The why usually reveals itself. Ask someone the date. It's a good start.

After that, we need to focus on finding Katie. Also, and I know this is strange… find out your name. It's probably not Tim." He gave his friend a crooked smile.

"Right. Didn't I hear that fellow call you Duncan, though?"

"Yes. Stands to reason we're likely our ancestors. I wouldn't be surprised if your surname is Buchanan. I'd guess I'm Arthur Duncan."

Tim frowned. "I'll be known as Graham, then. That was my relative, father of two boys killed in the bombing. Let's get on with it, then." He was clearly rattled, but John was relieved to see his friend at least willing to carry on. It would make matters far better if they could work together sensibly, rather than John having to do all of the heavy lifting.

They went back to their shift. John found the work strangely easy work, as though he'd been doing the work all his life. He assumed Arthur had been, so it made a certain sort of sense. He'd initially thought they'd been building a ship; in fact, he found they were doing repairs. The men all referred to him as "Duncan," which didn't help him nail down that his name was Arthur.

Eventually, he and Tim found their shift had ended. They started walking away from the shipyard, though John wasn't sure where he was meant to go. He had no idea where he called home.

They waited until they were somewhat more alone, and Tim confidentially informed him, "I have it. We're in 1941, early days in the war. It's March 10. That only gives us three days before the bombings start again. Well... for the first time. I don't know what you'd call it properly."

Tim had turned pale, and at the thought of being trapped in the middle of an entire city with bombs being rained down upon it was, John had to admit, terrifying for him as well.

"Well... is there anything that could have been done differently? Something that would have changed history?"

Tim nodded. "Many things. A bit of warning for one. There were too many false alarms leading up to the day, so people didn't take it seriously. Then there's the RAF."

"RAF?"

"The Luftwaffe weren't expected to fly so low, but they did. Air defenses were scrambled to combat them, yet were given orders to stay at an altitude…"

"Wait." John interrupted. "How do you know all of this?"

Tim gave a morose laugh. "Documentary. I've seen it a few times. But finishing my thought, the planes had to stay far above the bombers, and were unable to engage them. Stupid orders, but it was intended to keep the planes from being damaged by the bombings as well. Of course, if they knew they were coming, well. That would be entirely different."

"They could engage them early." John agreed.

"Right. They'd bombed London, Portsmouth, Birmingham, and Liverpool prior to their attack on Scotland. We're at the upper range of what they can reach. Here it is." He looked up at a tenement row where Tim seemed to think his family lived. "I've got a plan. Let me say you've come up for supper and I'll have another family member take you home. Ideally, they know where you live. If I'm wrong, I'm wrong, but it's worth a try."

"Of course. Let's try it, at least."

Tim's family welcomed him home as though nothing were out of the ordinary, and his wife seemed to recognize John. "You'll be staying with us for supper, Mr. Duncan?" She asked pleasantly enough.

"It was my plan, but I'm recalling I need to head back. Sink needs to be fixed up."

She looked worried to hear this. "Well, you'd better be getting on. Curfew will be coming on soon."

"I confess I forget the way home from here." John suggested.

She looked surprised by his admission. "Gregory knows the way." Pointing to the couple's teen son. The boy nodded.

The pair set out at once, and before long John was thanking Gregory for his help before the lad ran back towards his own home. John was tempted to knock on the door, but realizing that- in theory- it was his own place, he decided to simply try the doorknob. The door was opened on its own and a middle-aged man looked down at him, annoyed.

"You've taken your own sweet time, Ronald."

A female voice called from the back of the close. "Arthur? Is Ronald home?"

"Our son is here, yes. Finally."

John's mind raced back to the plaque. He'd only seen one Duncan listed, Arthur. He wondered if Ronald and his mother had died as well, but without being listed. Whatever the case may be, he knew it wouldn't do any good to stand in the doorway wondering. He'd just have to try to find Katie the next morning.

Chapter 4

The Lady and The Brute

Glasgow, Scotland

March 10, 1941

John and Tim were having a bad day. Katie's day bordered on the nightmarish.

She woke standing before a kitchen countertop. She'd been in the midst of making soup, judging from the weak-looking vegetables she had been chopping. The shock of transition from present to past was enough that she nearly chopped her own finger off, rather than a carrot. As it was, she barely caught the tip.

"Damn it!" She screamed out, clutching her finger in pain.

A man was sitting at a small kitchen table in the corner reading a newspaper. As she turned to face him, he looked over his horn-rimmed glasses. His expression was hardly one of concern. "Careful! You bleed on the veg, there won't be any more. Can't afford fresh veg every day, you know."

She looked down at her bleeding fingertip, saw she was wearing an apron, and wrapped the finger in it. After a pause when the pain had subsided slightly, she ran it under the faucet. "I'll try to be more careful." Katie replied, a hint of irritation rising in her voice.

The man set the newspaper down and crossed the room. He was standing directly in front of her. She expected that the man must be the husband of the person she'd replaced. But instead of concern, he drew back his fist as though to punch.

The move was so sudden she flinched involuntarily. He smiled, relaxing his stance. "Mind your tongue, Winifred. I'll not have my wife speaking to me with that tone. Do it again, I'll give you reason to complain. Understood?"

She regarded the bully coolly. "Yes. I understand."

"Very good. Finish making our supper." He went back to his table, picking up the paper. "Go on now."

Katie turned her head, smiling to herself. This man, whoever he was, had no idea who he was messing with. She'd led a Caledonian tribe to victory over the Romans and stared down a Scottish laird determined to destroy a town. This wife-beater would be in for a surprise in the near future. But for now, she'd bide her time.

She risked a glance at the paper as she cooked. She couldn't see the date, but it was extremely clear from the headlines that Britain was at war. She suspected as much; she was in Scotland in World War II. But where was John? And Tim?

Eventually, she served their meager dinner and the man, whom she learned was named Norman, left her without a compliment or comment to cleanup. He'd left the newspaper, and the date confirmed her fears. In days, Clydebank would be reduced to rubble.

Each time she'd time-hopped, there had been a purpose to her move. It seemed her purpose here was obvious, to stop the bombings. But it seemed strange to her that she'd be in such a strange position; a woman trapped living with a cruel husband. What did that have to do with the bombings?

When the dishes were washed, she went through all of the things in the kitchen, looking for clues regarding their circumstances. She found a letter. It appeared that she was Mrs. Norman Tavish of Glasgow. She recalled the street listing was on the west side of the city, towards Clydebank. It seemed she wasn't so far from where she'd started off, which she considered to be a good start.

Further searching found car keys. It was useful to know they had a car. As she dug around their things, Norman came in, donning a hat and coat. He sneered down at her with amusement.

"If I didn't know better, I should say you were looking for something."

"Nothing important, dear. You're off?"

"Of course."

"When will you be back?" His face grew stern, so she quickly added, "I shouldn't like to keep the lights on too late."

"Of course not. I'll not be gone an hour."

"All right."

She breathed a sigh of relief when he'd left. It gave her more time to search for useful information that might help her figure out what to do next. She started with their bedroom, looking for personal information. Their marriage license indicated her name prior to marriage had been Winifred Cathcart, her own maiden name. It confirmed her suspicion that she was inhabiting a relative's life; she didn't recall anyone named Winifred Cathcart in her family tree, but it wasn't impossible. She had done a lot of family research for the previous book. There had been hundreds of names, and if she'd married, all the more reason not to know of her.

There wasn't an endless amount of time before he returned, so she carried on with her search. By the time she had reached the attic, she thought to check her watch. Only another ten minutes. Katie glanced around, seeing hat boxes, crates and the like. Nothing of interest. She was about to go, when something about the floor caught her eye.

"Now that's odd." She took a closer look. There were footprints in the dust, likely Norman's from the size. They seemed to lead towards the far wall. "That's odd and that's impossible." She traced half a footprint, one that seemed to have partially disappeared within the wall itself.

She pressed against the wall, but it didn't give. "Clearly leads into something. There's got to be a door." Katie told herself. But a glance at her watch warned her she had little time. She felt around trying to discover a crack. As she was certain she'd found it, she followed the outline with her finger until she discovered a small notch in the wood she could just stick her finger into. It allowed her to swing open the door and look inside.

It was a very small room, just large enough for a desk and chair. On the desk was an extremely large radio, and on the wall she could see a shelf filled with notebooks. There was no time to look though; downstairs she heard a door slam.

"Winnifred!" Norman bellowed. "Put the kettle one."

She scrambled to close the door and exit the attic. She had barely closed the entrance when she spied him looking up at her from the stairwell. "Well?" He demanded.

"Right away, dear, of course."

Katie did as asked, wondering all the time what she'd stumbled onto. A secret radio. Who was Norman talking to? Why would he need to keep it so secret, even from his wife? She decided on a course of action. She'd sneak up to the attic again after he'd gone to bed, look through the notepads, take the car and go to Clydebank. She had no idea where John was, but she strongly suspected that he was either there or could be met there. Just as she had settled on what to do, Norman entered the kitchen. She involuntarily shivered at the sight of the nasty man.

"Yes?" She asked, trying to sound solicitous.

"You went upstairs again. To the attic, where I specifically asked you not to go." He slowly approached her, and she thought she spotted a long knife in his hands. "Dear Winifred, such a shame. I had hoped you'd obey me in this. But I see you leave me little choice."

Chapter 5

The Spy Exposed

Glasgow, Scotland
March 10, 1941

As Norman was closing in with his knife, she took a rapid mental stock of her available weapons. Without pause, she reached behind herself, grabbed the tea kettle, and hurled it at him. It opened somewhat on impact, spilling boiling water over his face.

The man shrieked and recoiled. It gave her a moment to look about her for anything she could defend herself with. She spotted the knives a moment before he could lunge for her.

Grabbing a steak knife, she dodged as he barely missed her. It was mostly instinctual, but she thrust forward with her own knife, striking him in the neck as he passed. The man opened his mouth, gaping in horror, then slid to the kitchen floor, dead.

"Dear God. Dear God." She cried, horrified. Katie dropped the knife and it clattered to the ground. But he had attacked her, hadn't he? And the radio was certainly suspicious. Everything about it was wrong, and matters had been forced upon her. She shook off her feelings, focusing instead on doing as she had intended.

She ran upstairs and hurried back to the secret radio room.

Looking over the radio, she had no clue how it worked. It was too confusing, so she grabbed the notebooks and took them downstairs.

On the sitting room sofa, she scanned through the books. They were filled with code, much as she feared. Almost none of the notation was useful to her, so she folded them up and put her head in her hands, thinking.

"The body. Better hide that." She found a door in the kitchen led to the cellar. She grabbed the corpse under the arms and pulled him to the stairs, then rolled him down. Once he was down there, she dragged him behind a few barrels so he wouldn't be very visible to someone who happened to look for him.

Back upstairs, she grabbed the car keys. "Enough time wasted here. Time to go to Clydebank."

***

It was dark by the time she'd reached the city. There was only one inn, so far as she could tell, so she booked herself a room and asked for a phone directory.

The directory gave her the address for an Arthur Duncan. She rang him up.

"Arthur Duncan here. Can I help you?" The man answered. He sounded nothing like John.

"Sorry. Wrong number." She hung up, frustrated. Looking through the directory, it occurred to her that each household was listed by the head only. It was always possible there was another family member. She decided she would try stopping by in the morning.

Alone in her room, she reviewed the notepads, hoping for a break. "Anything would be good at this point." She muttered to herself.

"Well well. What's this?" The very last notepad had what she was hoping for. "A key. Brilliant. I suppose he thought he was being clever and would destroy it if there were any danger."

Using some of the free space in one of the books, she began transcribing. What she discovered shook her. "Exact locations for the fuel depot. Landmarks to help with the bombing. All manner of details for the Nazis. Well, not feeling even the slightest hint of guilt at all now." She found herself saying. Katie had been forced to kill to survive as a Caledonian; removing a Nazi-collaborator from the war was surprisingly easier for her the more she reflected on it. The thought of the hundreds or possibly thousands who were still at risk from the bombs kept her mind focused on the necessity of her actions.

But when the lights were out and she was alone with her thoughts in the dark, the terrible image of the man sputtering and dying on the kitchen floor kept replaying all the same. She surprised herself by crying as she kept seeing the same image over and over again.

***

Clydebank, Scotland
March 11, 1941

It was early morning when she was standing at the door of the Duncan's, trying her best to look calm and composed. Katie hadn't slept hardly at all the night before, so she hoped she didn't look too terribly out of sorts.

A woman in her fifties answered the door, and she was plainly not happy to see her. "Yes? What do you want?" She asked, biting off each word as she spoke. It was a little after dawn, so Katie understood how she felt.

"I'm so, so sorry to be here this early. I was wondering... do you by any chance have a son, someone living with you other than your husband? I was afraid he might leave for work before I could see him."

The woman eyed her suspiciously. "Who wants to know?"

There seemed no point in giving her Winifred identity. "I'm Katie. Katie Cathcart. I met this fellow at a dance, and I wasn't sure where I could find him. We didn't exchange information." She'd practiced the excuse in the morning before leaving, and hoped it sounded more natural to the other woman than it did to her.

The woman rolled her eyes. "You mean Ronald. Wait here." She left Katie standing on the doorstep, clearly disapproving of the way the younger woman was conducting her affairs. Katie chuckled to herself; it did seem odd, she had to admit, but there wasn't a day to waste. The bombing would begin in 48 hours. Everything she saw would be turned into piles of cinder and ash if they didn't move quickly.

She was relieved to see John tucking in his shirt as he came down the stairwell, following the woman who thought she was his mother. John saw her as well, his eyes brightening. It was all she could do to stop herself from crying out and throwing herself into his arms.

"Hello! Oh, I don't know if you remember me, we met at the dance last week." She explained quickly, giving him a chance to know her excuse and play along. "I'm Katie Cathcart."

"Ronald Duncan." He extended a hand and smiled slyly, acknowledging the agreed upon excuse for seeing one another. "Won't you come in?"

"I'll fry up some eggs for breakfast, then." His mother said. She seemed to have softened in attitude from when they'd met. Though she still didn't approve of the timing, it seemed the older woman at least recognized the chemistry between the two when she saw it. "Don't be long, Ronald. You have work to ready for."

When they were sure they were out of her sight, John and Katie embraced, kissing quietly in the cramped entryway. "Why does this keep happening to us, John?" She whispered into his ears.

"I don't know. I wish I did, believe me, I do."

She nodded and drew away from him before Mrs. Duncan could return. "When can we meet?"

"Right after work." He told her that he and Tim worked at the docks. She drew in her breath sharply.

"It's one of the targets. The whole city is, actually. Let's meet then. I have a lot to show you. And a lot to do between now and then."

~ The Forbidden Rescue ~

Chapter 6

The Hotel Room

Clydebank, Scotland
March 11, 1941

Katie had fallen asleep for only ten minutes, she reckoned, as she'd tried to transcribe as fast as she could. Norman had been incredibly active in gathering data to share with the Germans. She wondered if he was part of a cell, a group who had been traveling about to get the information. It seemed unlikely that given he was in Glasgow, he'd been able to radio direct to, say, the French Coast. Likely he'd had collaborators. If so, she felt pleased that she'd disrupted at least one aspect of the group.

She'd managed to transcribe nearly two of the five notebooks worth of information. Katie had quickly filled the blank space she'd had and been forced to go out to buy more paper. It had been a wonder to her as she'd gone on her errand for a sandwich and more materials, to see how remarkably close the residential buildings were packed in next to industrial sites. Within the crowded, booming city- far more booming than it had been in 2019- she had witnessed crowds of people in the industrial, northern town going about their business for lunch, work, and school. It was alarming to think that very soon a large number of these people would be dead or wounded.

She saw the baffle walls Tim had described, and it was fairly clear that there were at least some shelters from bombs. The town wasn't entirely unprepared. But it wasn't going to be enough, not by a long sight.

When evening fell, she waited patiently for Tim and John to arrive at the hotel, still writing away even as her hand cramped from the effort. When they knocked, she was briefly startled; she'd been so engrossed in transcribing, she hadn't expected to jump. She had anyway.

"Hello beautiful." John greeted her with a kiss as he and his friend entered her small room. "What have you found out?"

"Plenty. Far too much, really." She explained the extent of the intelligence she'd discovered. "We need to turn this over to the authorities."

"Who? Military? Police?" Tim asked, skeptically as he looked over the materials. "What are they even going to do with it? Why would they believe us, either?"

"I'll tell them the truth." Katie replied, feeling defensive. "My husband- I hate calling that scum that, but it's necessary- was a spy for Germany. Here's his notebooks. They can check out our apartments and see the radio for themselves."

John nodded his agreement. "We've got to do something! We can't just stand by with this. It's worse than doing nothing."

Tim thought about it. "Fine. Let's skip work, go first thing in the morning. Then I think we'd be wise to leave town. Get out before disaster strikes."

"How do we get your families out, though? Tim, you have family here?"

He nodded. "A wife, two sons. They all died in the Blitz."

"And John, you have family. I met your mother. How do we convince them to leave?"

He shook his head. "It won't be easy. We need to come up with something. I imagine it would be easier for you, though, Tim."

"Right. Man of the house, and all that rubbish. I suppose I could just tell them we're going to go and be done with it."

Katie nodded. "We'll work on John's parents. Go home now, we'll meet back in the morning. We can take what we have to the military then and hope for the best."

After bidding them farewell, John and Katie were left alone. "You should get home too. Your parents will be worried."

He smirked. "Well, I do think it's okay if I stay out in your company a bit longer, don't you?"

She grinned. "Perfect. I need someone to help me with the transcriptions."

He groaned. "That seems like a lot of work. Are you sure?"

"Yes. But we can take a break for a bit. I've been at this all day." She yawned. "Most of all, I could use a back-rub."

"That I can do for you."

Katie laid down on the bed and relaxed as John ran his hands across her back, massaging the tension out of her muscles. When he worked his way down to her legs, she sighed. "Perfect."

"You sure?"

"Absolutely." She assured him. Katie flipped over. "Front."

"Yes ma'am." He grinned, rubbing her stomach.

As he moved his way down to her thighs, she reached up to touch his face. She guided his head down to her stomach, which he began to kiss slowly, licking the belly button and playfully moving its way towards her panties. As she touched his muscular shoulders, he pulled her skirt and panties down and started to lick her.

As he licked her more intensely, she began to moan. Katie's hand strayed down to his pants, unzipped him, and pulled his hardened rod out. She slowly stroked him as his tongue moved in and out of her.

Katie glided out of her clothing, and as she did John stripped down as well. She slipped off the bed and bent before him. "From here. I want it like this." She insisted. John stepped behind her and after positioning himself, slowly moved into her. As he drove into her, she closed her eyes and reaching down, touched herself.

"Now!" She cried out, feeling the excitement rising. "Come on, now, baby!"

Together, their pleasure reached a climax and release. They were left panting and happy.

"Where did that even come from?" She asked as they curled up on the bed. "How are we in the mood with everything that's been going on?"

"I don't know." He admitted. "It's hard to say. I feel like it's because we feel stronger together in these situations. Our love was saved in Caledonia, after all."

"True." She agreed. "But I mean, you know... the war..."

"There was a war then too. In some ways it was even more personal. You saw the face of the person who was going to kill you. Though, I suppose if you see the pilot, it would be much like what we saw when fighting the Romans."

Katie snuggled in close to him under the covers, resting her head against his chest. "I feel like we shouldn't have done this though. It feels wrong."

John sighed. "It's life-affirming. I think when you're surrounded by this much grimness and horror, you want to connect with life."

She yawned. "Set the alarm for four hours from now. I can't write another thing, and my hand needs to rest from all the writing I did early today. We can sleep for a bit and then we really need to finish the transcription. Or, at least as far as we can."

He agreed and set the alarm. As they drifted off to sleep, Katie hoped she could keep the image of the stabbing out of her mind. And though at first it didn't seem like it would happen, exhaustion overtook her.

Chapter 7

Day of the Bombers

Clydebank, Scotland
March 12, 1941

Tim and the Duncans were driving up to the airbase the next day. Katie sat in the passenger seat, rubbing her hand and wincing.

"You are seriously my heroine, Katie." Tim said. "You really transcribed over three of those full books?"

"Yes. I won't write a word for another week, at least."

"I believe it. And here we are." They approached the base and two armed men approached their windows. One tapped on the glass as Tim rolled down his window.

"ID."

"We're not expected." Tim started. "We have…"

"Turn around the vehicle, sir, and leave immediately."

He shook his head. "You don't understand. We need to speak to your base commander."

The man shook his head. "No one goes in or out without clearance. Turn the car around now. I must insist."

Katie leaned forward and gave the man her most charming smile. "Sir? I discovered my husband is a Nazi spy. I have the proof here. Can I speak with your superior?"

The soldier's jaw dropped. "What? Ma'am, you're surely joking."

"Afraid not."

He considered what he was being told. "Wait here." After a quick trip to the guardhouse, he returned at a quick pace. "Drive forward. You're to report to the first building to the left. You'll be escorted, so wait there."

The three were taken to the base commander, a white-mustachioed

Colonel Harrington, who reviewed their offered material with a grim, unfriendly stare. "You bring this to me and claim we'll be attacked tomorrow? You're certain?"

"We are." Katie promised.

"I'll review this material and consider it. Thank you, good day." Colonel Harrington yawned, dismissing the group.

"But- wait." Katie said, shocked by his attitude. "Aren't you going to read any of it? Don't you have any questions? For instance, we know they're coming in low, very low. They'll be so low your fighters won't be able to engage. People need to be warned, and there's no time!"

He scoffed. "That's perfectly fine. I appreciate that you've brought this to me. You've told me where to find you. This is all here, correct? It's all I need for now. Now, if you don't mind I have many duties to attend to today. Good day."

This time he got up and showed them out. But as he was doing so, he failed to see Katie pocket an item from his desk.

As they left and drove back into town, Katie was furious. "This is ridiculous! We've done everything we were supposed to, and we've gotten nowhere."

John tried to calm her. "He said he'd review it."

"He has no intention of reviewing anything! The bastard didn't take us seriously. We've got to do something!"

"Right." Tim agreed. "But what would that be?"

Katie smiled. "Oh, I have something in mind. The alarm. We need to set it off early so people have a chance to get underground."

John nodded slowly. "We could do that, if we can convince them they're supposed to do so. But what about getting our families out of here?"

"We need to do that too." Tim agreed. "We should take them out of here today."

"We can do that." John agreed. "And after we've got them safely away, we can come back and try to get the word out."

They started by going to Tim's house and dropping him off. "Take them up into the hills, into the country." John suggested. "They'll be safe there."

"I'll do that. Let's meet back at my place tomorrow. Agreed?"

"It's the best plan we've got." Katie said.

When they reached the Duncan house, his parents were less than thrilled to see them both. It was too early for John's shift to have ended. "You two have been off all day, to the cinema or wherever it is you go, Ronald, and shirking your duties. Now you say you want us all to run off into the country for two days? It's obscene! Don't you realize there's a war on?"

"I do. Trust me." John replied, trying to keep the tension out of his voice. "We need to take a break, though. I've been working a lot of hours and my supervisor said it was fine. This is the best time to get away and, well, I want to treat you and Mum. You've earned it."

Arthur Duncan started to protest, but his wife interrupted. "Now Arthur. Ronald is trying to do something nice for us. It's not often he can do that, now is it?"

"No, I suppose not."

"Then let's pack!"

**

Clydebank, Scotland
March 13, 1941

"You're absolutely certain this is the instruction?"

"Yes." John told the man at the early warning center for the fourth time. "You have documentation to prove it."

"It does look good. Very well."

Katie, Tim, and John left the building as it was starting to grow dark. "We're ready to leave town? There's nothing more we can do, right?" John mused.

"Yes. That was good thinking, Katie, taking the Colonel's stamp off the desk. Without it, I doubt we'd have convinced them to issue the air raid warning early. They think it's a drill, and ideally people won't make that same assumption."

"If we can just get people to pay attention and head towards safety, that's something." Katie suggested. "So let's- wait. Where's the car?"

They had parked nearby, but the car Katie had taken from Glasgow was now missing. She started to shake with fear. "Stolen. Someone stole our car and we only have an hour before the bombs fall."

"What in hell!" Tim shouted, looking around in horror. "This is a disaster. We need to get out of here now, right now. What do we do?"

"Run?" Katie suggested.

They began to do exactly as she suggested, sprinting down the street, Tim leading the way. "Are we going the right way?" Katie yelled.

"Yeah, towards Glasgow! Keep going!"

They kept at it until they were completely out of breath. Even so, they were still too far from the outskirts to be safe from the attack when it was finally dark. Even though the sun was down, they could see well enough thanks to the moonlight. The sirens were going off, and the last few people on the streets ran for cover.

"What do we do?" Tim asked.

Katie scanned the street, pointing to a theater. "That way."

"There? Why?" Tim asked.

"Because they probably have a basement." John finished, picking up on Katie's idea. He took her by the hand and they fled for the building.

The door had been left open, so they ran in. The building looked empty at first, but Katie found a door leading to the basement. "This way! Come on!"

John was the last one to the door, and as he was about to slam it shut, he heard planes overhead. "It's here. They're here."

He managed to get to the bottom of the stairs when the first concussion rocked the building. Katie, Tim, and John found they weren't alone; there were dozens of children and their parents already there, huddled against the walls.

"Did we make any difference? Didn't it work at all?" Katie asked. As she asked, she was shocked to find she was yawning. Tim slumped over.

"Wait… now? It's happening now?" She barely had time to say as the darkness enveloped her. The last thing she saw was a frightened child being held by her mother. She thought briefly that it seemed unfair she could escape the situation and the child could not, but had no further thoughts as she disappeared into the dark.

~ The Forbidden Rescue ~

Chapter 8

Home at Last

Clydebank, Scotland

March 10, 2019

Katie pointed down to the plaque in the park where the trio had just re-awoken. "Just twenty names. Unbelievable."

"Not a Duncan or a Buchanan amongst them. Mostly pilots, it looks like." Tim noted. "It's hard to believe the Colonel took us seriously. He didn't seem like he was going to at all."

"Well, he did." Katie said with a smile. "The fighters must have intercepted most of the bombers before they could reach the town."

"So... is there even an assignment now?" John wondered. He checked his smartphone and smiled. "First time I've ever been glad to lose a gig. There's no messages from my employer. Apparently, this is a non-story as the town wasn't seriously damaged."

Katie wrapped her arms around him. "We're good. I don't care if we get thrown out of the house. We're alive and we saved so many lives!"

They walked over to their car, ready to go home. But before they could leave, Tim pointed across the street. "What's that?"

"What?" John asked, then looked much closer. "That shop. Does it say Duncan's?"

"It does. Should we check it out?" Tim asked.

They crossed the street and walked in. The high-end clothing store was fairly busy, and a young female employee approached immediately. "Hello. Can I be of serv- oh! Mr. and Mrs. Duncan! What an honor to have you here. We weren't expecting you."

Katie and John shared a confused look. "We- well, sure." John responded. "We just thought we'd drop in while we were in town. You know. Just, um, dropping in."

"Very good. If there's anything at all that you need, please let me know. I'm the head sales clerk." The woman said.

After they'd left, John scratched his head. "So- what was that?"

Katie began scrolling through her smartphone, doing on-the-spot research. "Arthur Duncan was a tailor.

It seems he started a department store in 1942. After the war, it took off. Oh my God." She exclaimed, looking at the website. "He died rich. One of the richest men in Scotland."

"Hmm." John looked down the road. "An ATM. Shall we?"

They checked their account and John laughed in shock. "It seems Arthur's money didn't leave the family. We're apparently not going to need to work ever again unless we want to. Ever again, unless we just decide to start throwing millions away on Caribbean islands."

***

Katie and John drove back to Dungallow mostly in silence. First, they'd dropped Tim off with family members in Clydebank, the children of Graham who had survived the war. He'd promised he'd meet back up with them in Dungallow to talk about their experiences. "I'll catch a cab or a bus back, or something."

"You're sure?" John asked. "Because honestly... I guess we could buy another car. We have absolutely no shortage of money."

Tim laughed. "Ah, don't start spending your money like the multi-millionaires you are just yet. Get used to the idea. Besides, I like the car you have now, don't you know. No need to trade it in just yet."

As they entered the village, Katie crossed her arms and sighed as she looked over their adopted town. "We have millions of dollars and we live in Scotland. It's great, but it's strange how our lives keep changing. I don't understand why this keeps happening to us. Can't we stop it?"

"I wish I knew how. We need to research it. Maybe we should put some of those millions to use in finding out why."

She nodded. "That and we could buy some fun things. I have something in mind."

John laughed. "Really? What were you thinking? A castle?"

"No, nothing so grand as that. Actually, I was thinking I might like to take a cruise, if you'd be up for that. It'd be a good place for my writing and it's something I've always wanted to do."

They pulled up to their bungalow. Nothing there had changed, they realized. The money in their account was the only sign that history had changed and made them rich. "Okay. Where do you have in mind? The Bahamas? The Med?"

Katie shook her head. "No, not exactly. I was thinking I'd like to take an around-the-world cruise."

"Really? We could."

They unlocked the door to their house and, both feeling exhausted, dropped down onto the couch next to each other. John put an arm around his wife. "Seriously, though, you'd like to do this? A trip like that would take a year, at least."

"I know. Make it a year then. We'll see all the ports of Africa, Asia, and the Americas before we come home. Really see the world. I've always wanted to know what it was like to sail the ocean. It's about the only really expensive thing I've ever wanted. I'd understand if you didn't want to do it, though."

He snickered. "And I'd be the biggest idiot in the world to pass that up. We're doing this. I can't wait!"

"Are you sure?"

"Absolutely, dear. Wherever you go, I go. Across centuries, wars, whatever it may be, I will always be by your side." John promised.

Katie kissed his cheek. "I know. You'd better be. I can't picture my life without you. Oh! And pictures. Think of the shots you'll score in Zanzibar and Taipei."

He nodded, stroking his chin and pretending to be evil. "That had occurred to me too. This is all about my career, you know."

They shared a laugh. "We have to stop time-traveling, though. I need that to end." Katie insisted.

"I know." John agreed. "But wherever you go, I'll go. I promise. I'll love you forever."

"I love you too, John. From now on, only in the present, though, right?"

He took her hand and kissed her once more. "Absolutely."

***

Preview of the next book in the series...

"Alone In Time"

Chapter 1

The Flag

Zanzibar, Tanzania

July 20, 2019

Stone Town was proving to be everything Katie had hoped it would be.

She and her husband strolled arm and arm through the historic quarter of Stone Town, or old town, on the island of Zanzibar. She knew very little about the island, but John was in rare form today, explaining the history of the Swahili port whether she wanted to hear it or not.

"That's why they essentially have two different governments. Well, not entirely different," He was saying as they wandered the marketplace. She could smell cooking meats, drying cloves, and the scent of other spices she didn't recognize. The tropical island lying off the coast of East Africa was enjoying a cool day, thanks to pleasant breezes floating in from the Indian Ocean. "Tanganyika, or the mainland, was once a German colony. Culturally, there's a distinct difference between…"

He stopped in the middle of the sidewalk, forcing the crowd of locals and tourists trailing behind to move around them.

"What?" Katie asked, worried.

"I'm… I'm rambling on and on again, aren't I?" John asked, sounding a little embarrassed.

She laughed. "Oh, honey, ramble all you like. I love the sound of your voice. Sometimes, I even listen to the words."

Her joke got him cracking up. If John was at times a bit of a bore with his impromptu history lessons, Katie appreciated that he at lEast had a self-deprecating sense of humor.

"I award you a C in Tanzanian history and an A+ for being an awesome wife." He declared as they started back on their walk.

"Fair marks, professor. That works for me."

Soon, they were leaning into the stalls and over tables in the marketplace, inspecting the wares on offer. Katie found she was mentally restraining herself from buying every unique piece of non-tourist trash that caught her eye. It had been a temptation to buy at every port they'd stopped at. They'd gone from being on the brink of losing their modest, rural cottage home to being multi-millionaires overnight. It was a disorienting life change, and though she really could afford to buy anything in the market that interested her, an even stronger pull towards keeping her sense of identity was at war within her. She brushed back her bright red hair as she considered how to deal with the problem, revealing the signature high cheekbones she was best known for among friends.

"See anything you want to bring home?" John asked. He'd shaved off the beard, to her relief, after their last adventure. She was grateful; she preferred him with smooth cheeks and close-cut hair. But she didn't want to dictate his look to him, so she had made it a policy not to mention her preferences.

"That's the trouble. Everything interests me. Carpets, clothes, handmade and decorated dishes... it's all too much. A little..." She slowly raised her hand, rubbing her sweating forehead and temples. "It's a little overwhelming."

"Oh! Hey, do you want to head back to the ship?"

"I don't want to ruin your good time." She protested.

John shrugged. "We have another day in port. Then we have the crossing ahead." Though piracy in Somalia had been largely eliminated in 2018, it still remained policy for cruise ships like the *Shadow of the seven seas* to sail as far afield from Somalia's shores as possible, for insurance purposes. Katie knew this because John had explained the situation, along with a number of other itinerary issues in passing before they set sail. Soon, they'd be in the middle of the Indian Ocean, far removed from the African coast.

Though she did tune him out when he tended to "ramble" as he put it, on this point she had paid close attention. The round-the-world cruise had been her idea, and she was interested in all aspects of itinerary.

But on the day Katie and John had boarded the ship, she felt anxiety rising inside her. Money changed people in meaningful ways. She had strongly valued the easy-going, uncomplicated way she and John approached life since their move to Scotland. It was a contrast to the unstable and strange events that had intruded into their life in recent years. It was the knowledge that they were just ordinary people pursuing creative careers that kept her anchored.

"You sure you're okay?" John asked after they'd traversed the gangway back on board. The passports for John and Katie Duncan had been checked thoroughly, and they were heading back to their suite.

It was the third time he'd asked. "Stop asking me that!" She snapped.

He took a step back. "Okay, fine. You don't have to bite my head off."

Katie walked away from her husband and gazed overboard, leaning slightly over the rail to look down. A drop from that height would have been several stories, and though she wanted to clear her head by looking to the sea, she didn't want to think about what would happen if someone fell. From her peripheral vision, she saw that John was starting to walk away.

It was Katie's turn to feel a little embarrassed. "Hold on. I'm just not myself. Sorry. I'm going to get some aspirin from the store, okay?"

"I can do that for you." He offered. His voice was still tense, but he was at lEast trying, and she appreciated it.

"No, hon." She kissed him quickly on the cheek. "Give me a little time to myself and to cool off. It's kind of a weird day for me. I'll see you in an hour, okay?"

"Sure. No problem." He returned her kiss, squeezing her hand as he took off for what she presumed would be the ship's library.

She went to the store, bought aspirin and a soda, and decided to stroll around the ship to kill time and relax. One of the things she liked about the ship's design was that the designers had scattered museum piece displays from each port the ship visited throughout the guest corridors and public areas. She'd tried to check them out on her own, patrolling from deck to deck and admiring what she saw, but the cruise ship was massive. She'd only gotten through a few decks on the trip since departing from Glasgow some weeks ago.

It was strange to her, still, to be an expatriate living between Scottish and American worlds. She reminded herself that her new British nationality was part of the overall tension that was affecting her mood. She and John had lived much of their lives in Chicago. But now that they were in their thirties, they had relocated to Dungallow, Scotland for reasons that many people considered unbelievable. She could relate to that feeling; if she hadn't lived it, she wouldn't believe it either.

As she had written in her first book, it seemed she and John had become the first known time-travelers in history. It wasn't a title they relished, and she felt her cheeks grow red every time she was questioned on the matter. Yet, it was an undeniable fact for her and John that they had gone back to live several months in Caledonian Scotland during a vacation some years ago. They'd time travelled after that only to find themselves in the midst of the Highland clearances. Most recently, they'd been forced to revisit the Clydebank Blitz of 1941. Their actions apparently held consequence; the history of the blitz had been altered, and they had returned to find themselves rich beyond their imaginings of wealth.

It was a lot to take in. Though she loved Scotland and now considered it to be her home, she did hope and expect to find that her unplanned journeys were at an end. This cruise was a trip entirely of her own making, one she was happy to plan and to set off on. At the lEast, it would keep her from the sort of artifacts that seemed to displace the couple in the time-space continuum.

She felt tired as she walked, and decided it was time for bed. But when she returned to the cabin, she saw John stretched out on the bed, fast asleep.

It was tempting to join him, but she thought she might sleep poorly with him next to her; he had become prone to tossing and turning in his sleep since they'd taken to sea, while she had never slept better. Being rocked to sleep each night was one of the high points of her experience. She gave him a quick, unseen smile, and turned away from her husband, softly closing the door behind her.

Realizing her headache had cleared, she opted to get a light supper at the Italian restaurant on one of the lower decks. She smiled as she thought about the stops and the cuisine she'd sampled; fine wine at a little café in Lisbon, lemon yassa in Dakar, a tasty stew called potjiekos in Cape Town. She reflected that it was a good thing she was running and working out each day in the ship's gym.

She tried to find her way to the restaurant and soon discovered she'd stepped off on the wrong deck. Instead of turning around right away, she quickly became immersed in checking out the Portuguese relics on display. The distraction was a welcome one before dinner.

As she was thinking about how long it would be before they reached India, the Pacific, and eventually America, she noticed that the Portuguese displays had ended and had turned British. The ship had stops after an initial trans-Atlantic departure from New York to Dublin, Glasgow, Liverpool, and Portsmouth prior to stops in France, Spain and Portugal. The British exhibits included a few stereotypically British naval pieces she expected amidst memorabilia from the Victorian and Edwardian eras. Strangely, she noted a tattered flag was located in the mix.

"Banner of the Duncan Clan, Undated," the plaque next to it read. Her breath caught. Here was a piece of her husband's family history! She had to bring him down to see it, she realized.

Then again- that might be a bad idea. The past three times they'd travelled back in time, they had been near objects associated with their family history. She had no desire for either of them to time travel. She resolved not to show him the object, just in case.

It was hard to even distinguish the coloration of the flag. She leaned forward to get a closer look and as she did so, she found herself yawning.

"No!" She shouted, staggering back. The panic rose inside as she recognized the first sign of time travel. Her vision blurred. Katie sat down hard and felt tears flooding her sight.

"I can't! No, not now!" But her final words were slurred, and she slumped over in the corridor.

***

Grab your copy of

"Alone In Time"

Available on Amazon or at a store near you. Liked what you've read? Check out other books available from SubArctic Publishing on Amazon.

About the Author

From Scotland to Egypt, South America to Japan - travel the world in romance. William Newell enjoys creating imaginative novellas which are captivating. Come home each evening and explore a deep relationship between animated characters while learning the history of a new part of the world.

William is passionate about creating deep connections between the characters in his works to bring them alive off the page, while adding a modern twist to their everyday obstacles. Expect humor and whit while living the adventure in the richly detailed canvas of these stories.

His goal is to enrich and entertain, providing an avenue of enjoyment which sparks the creativity and imagination of his readers. Besides writing, William's passion is learning about the history of the world's most unique cultures. He aims to weave his own knowledge into each individual story he creates.

Visit William Newell's Author Page on Amazon.

Made in United States
North Haven, CT
15 November 2021